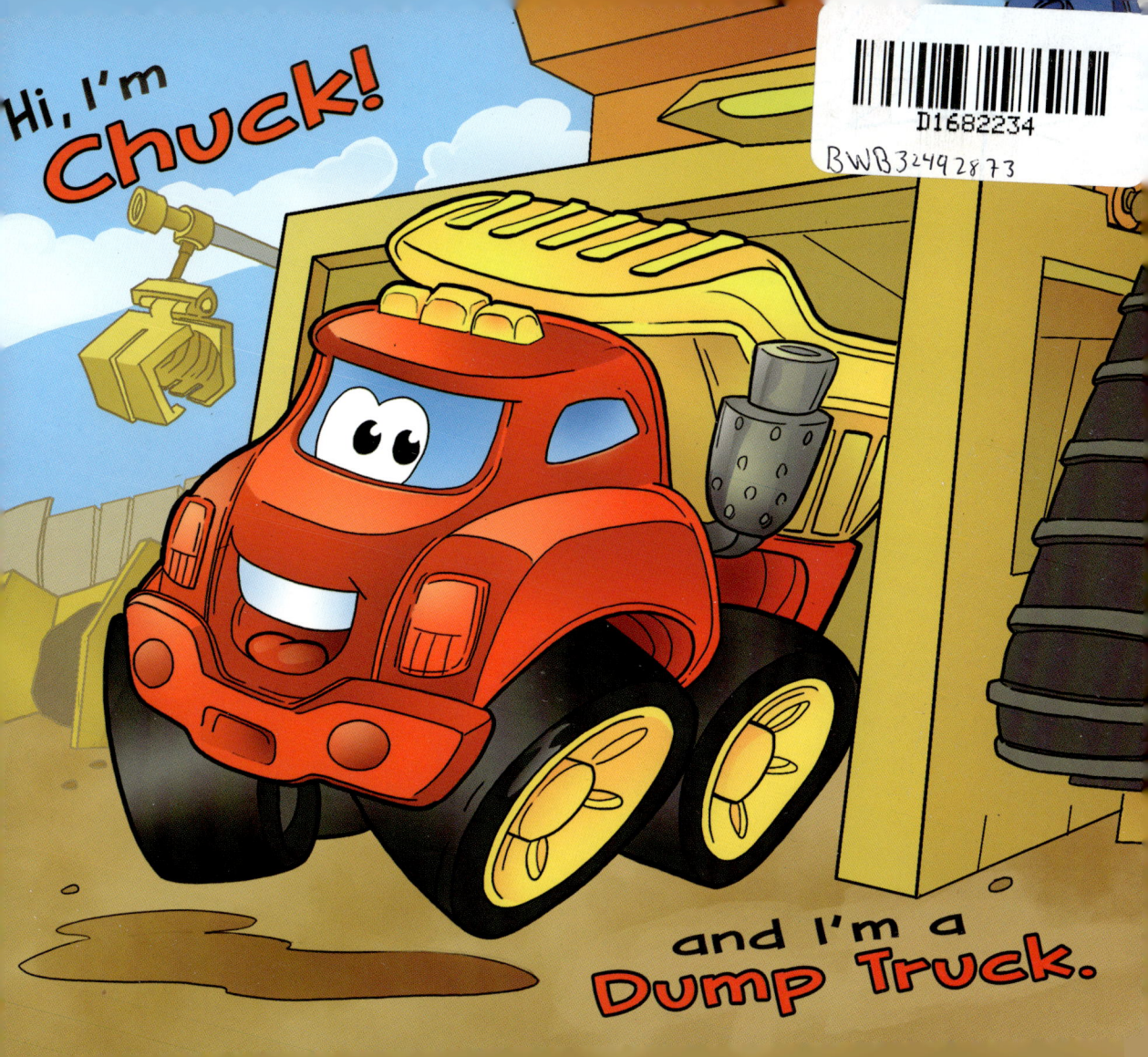

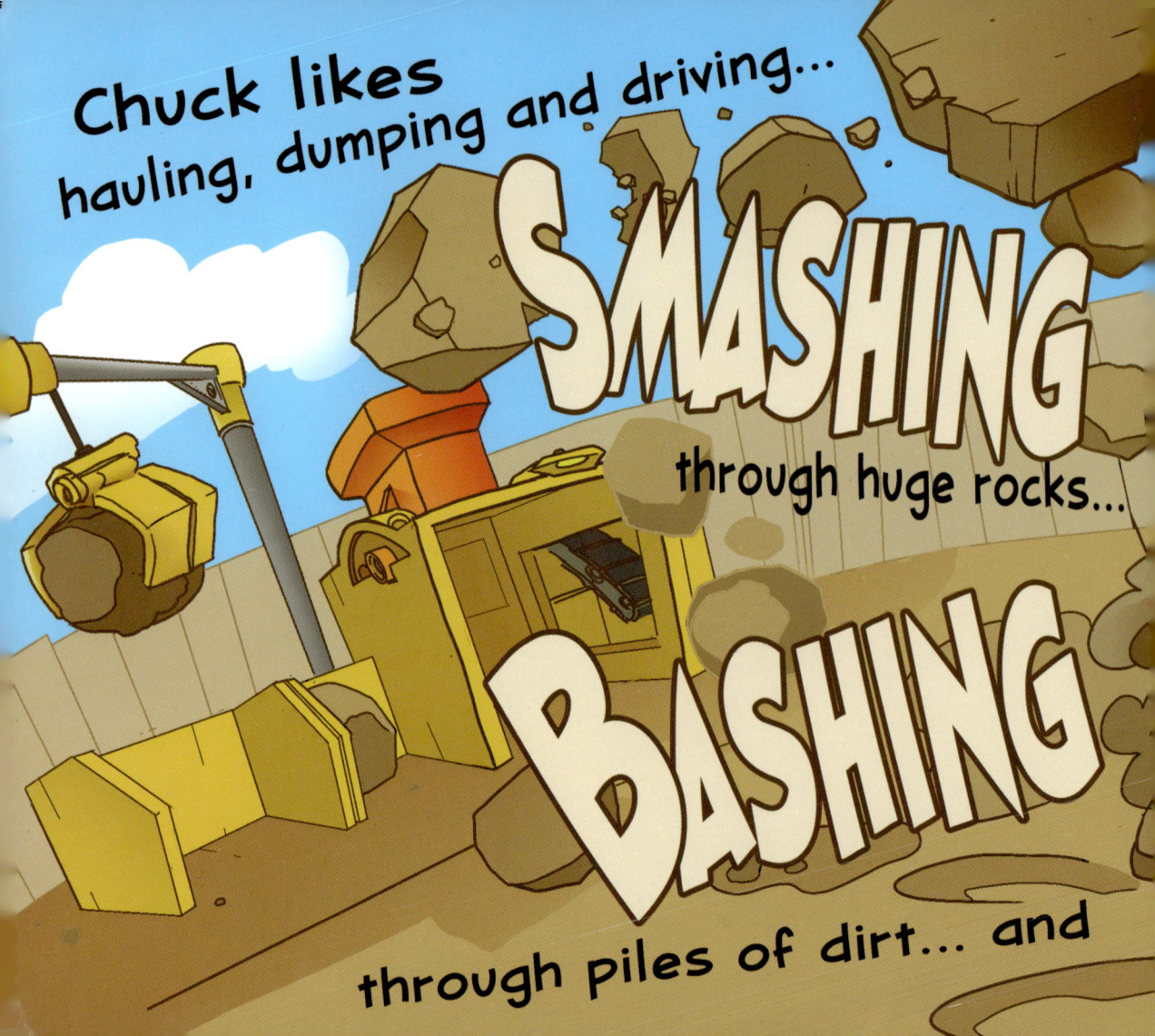

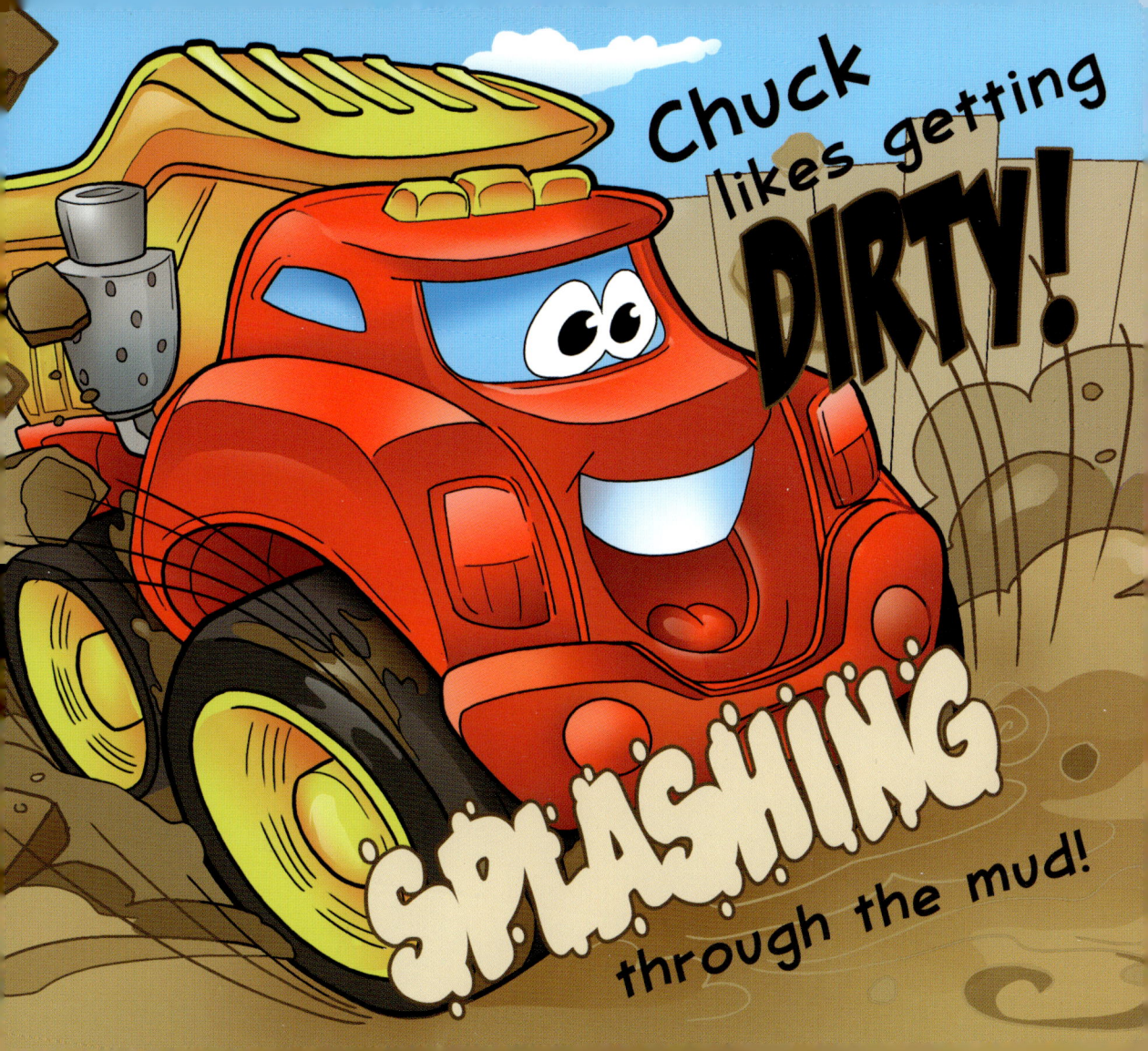

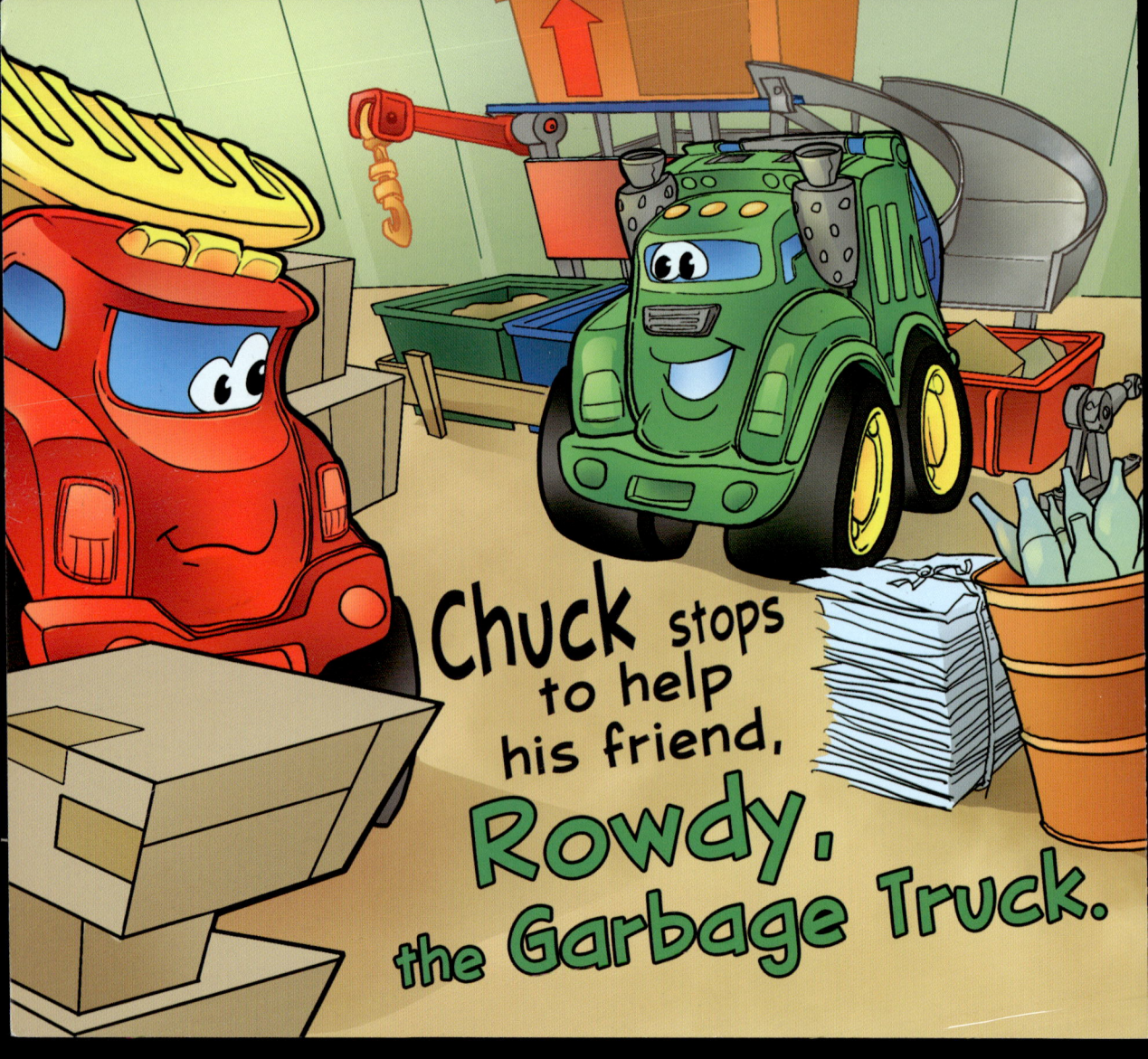

Chuck stops
to help
his friend,
Rowdy,
the Garbage Truck.

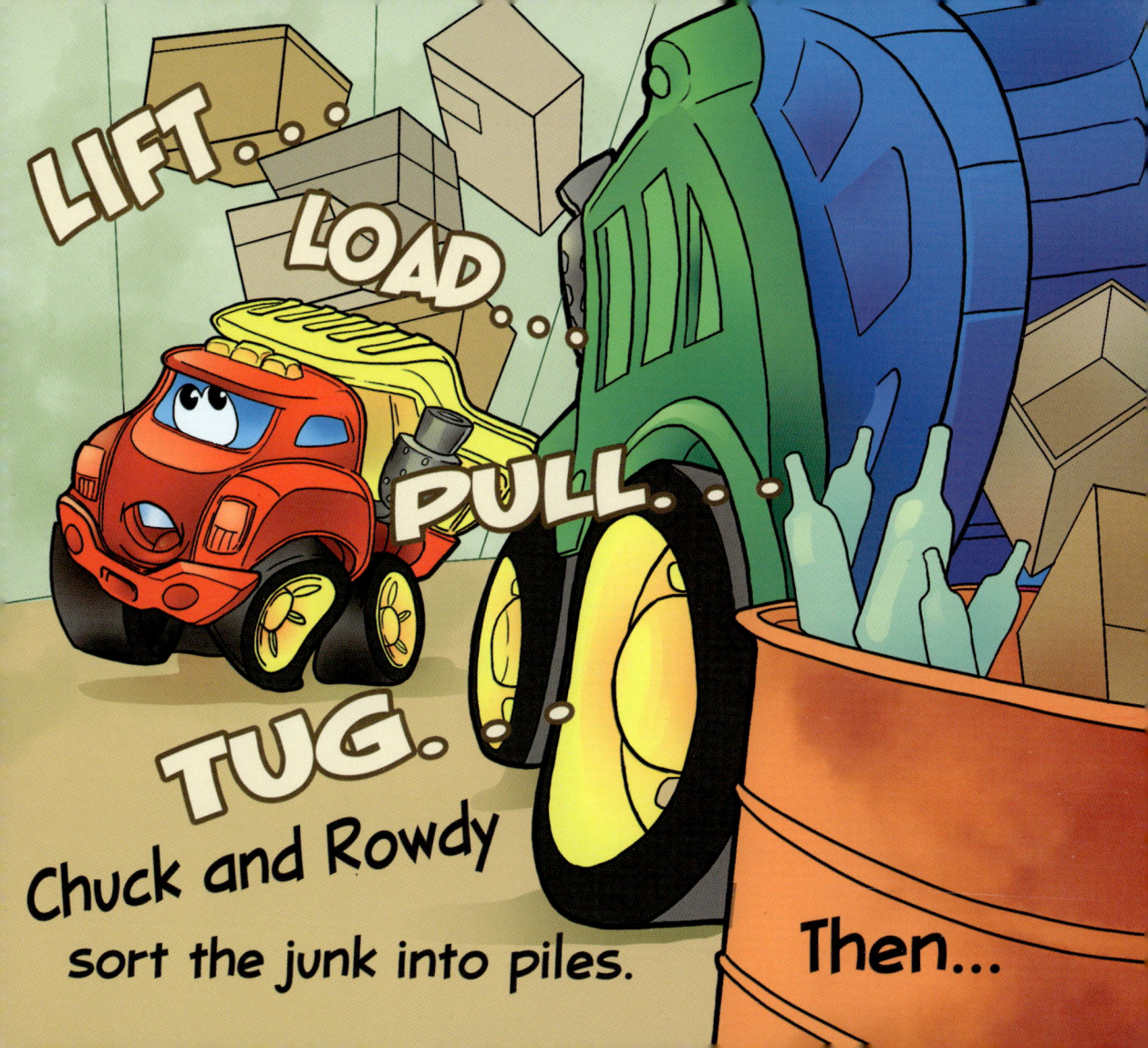

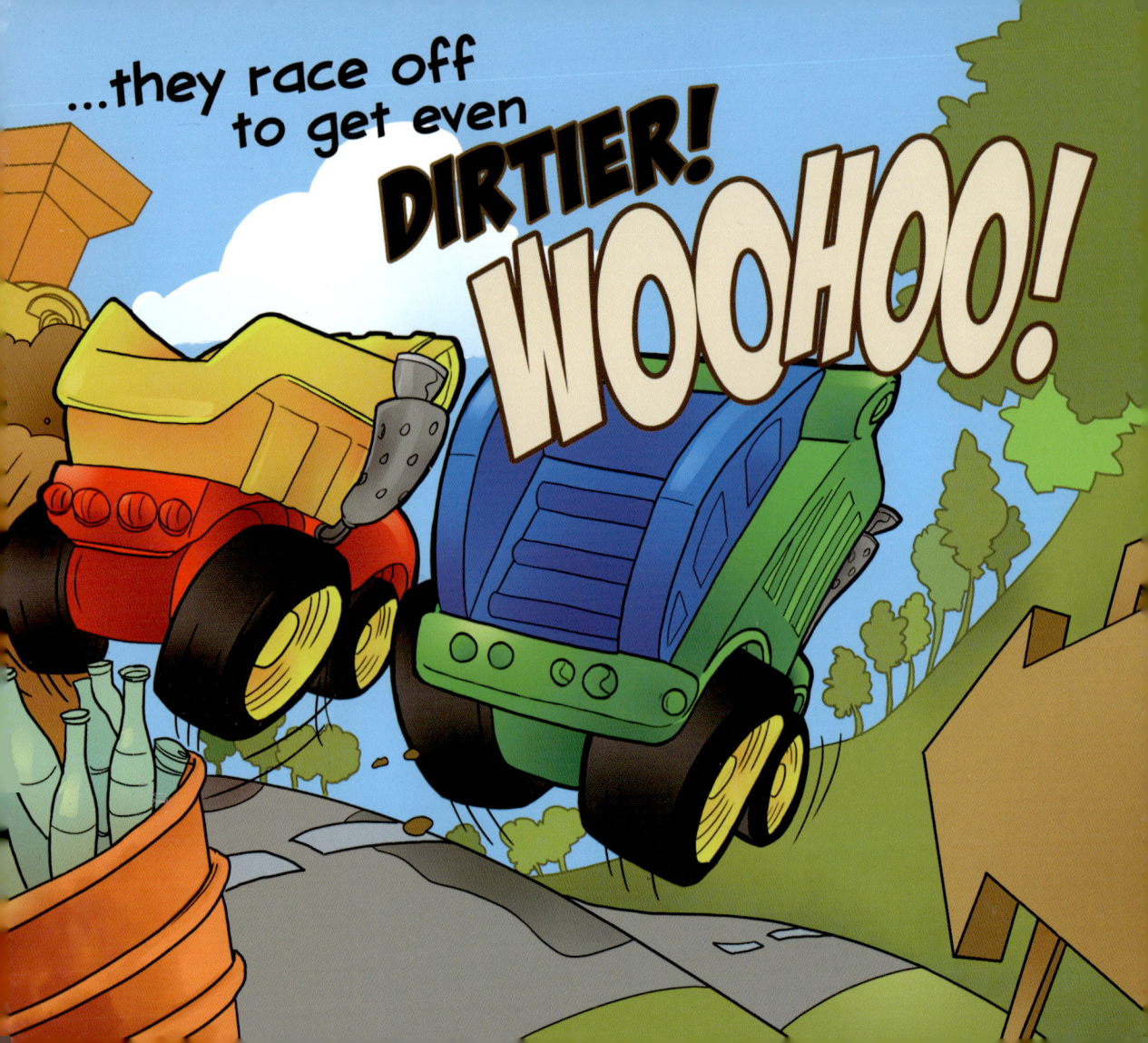

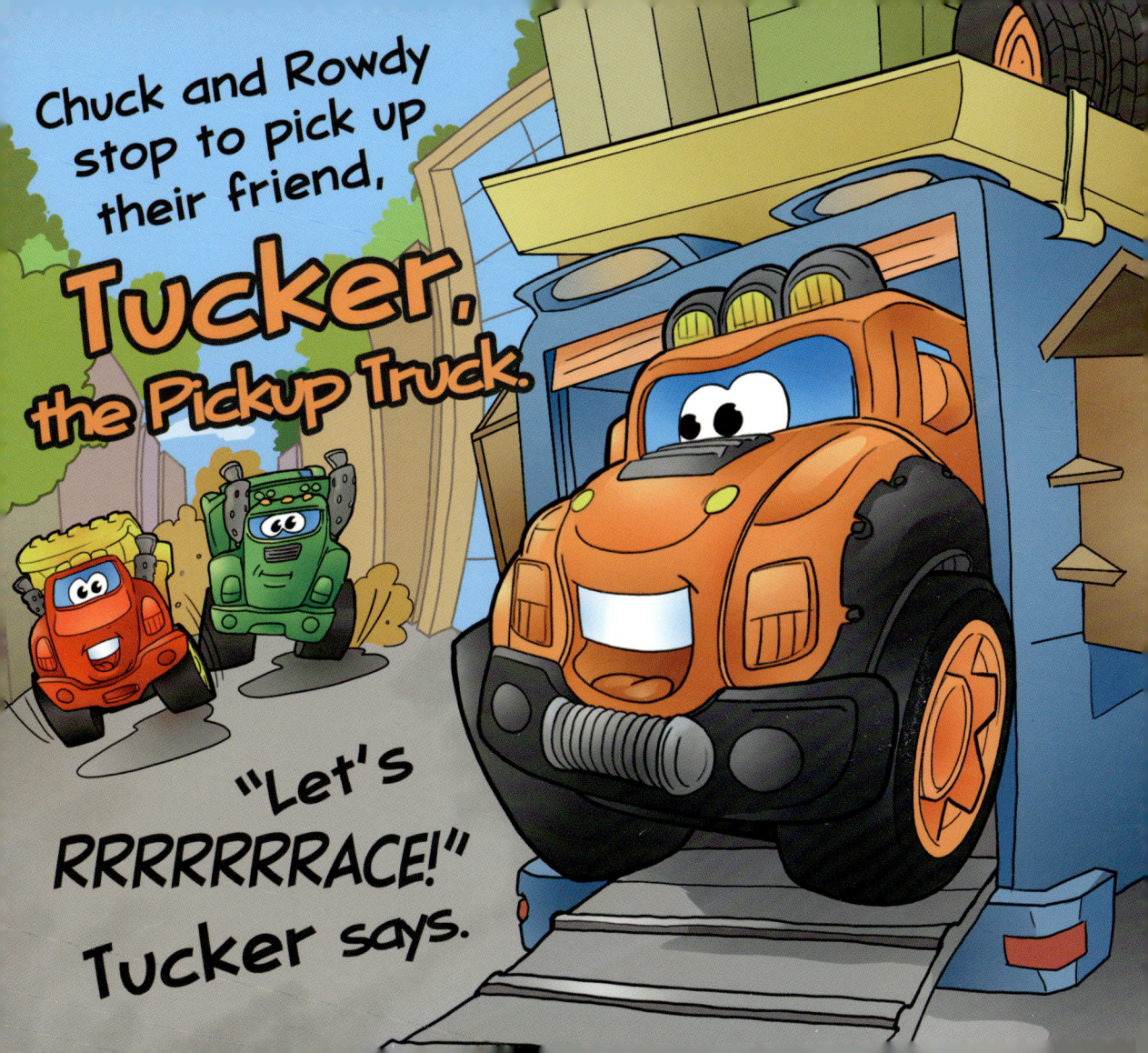

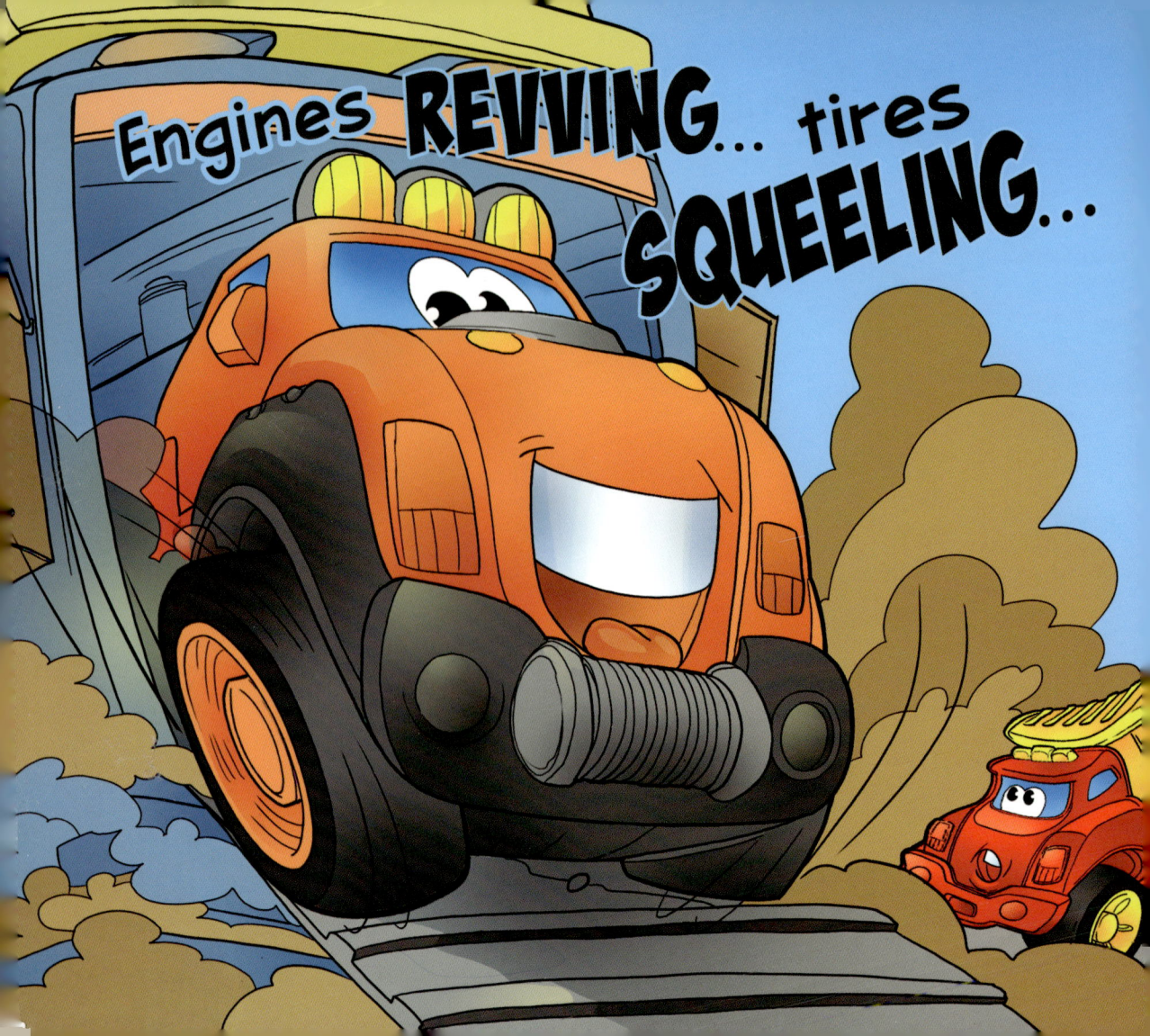

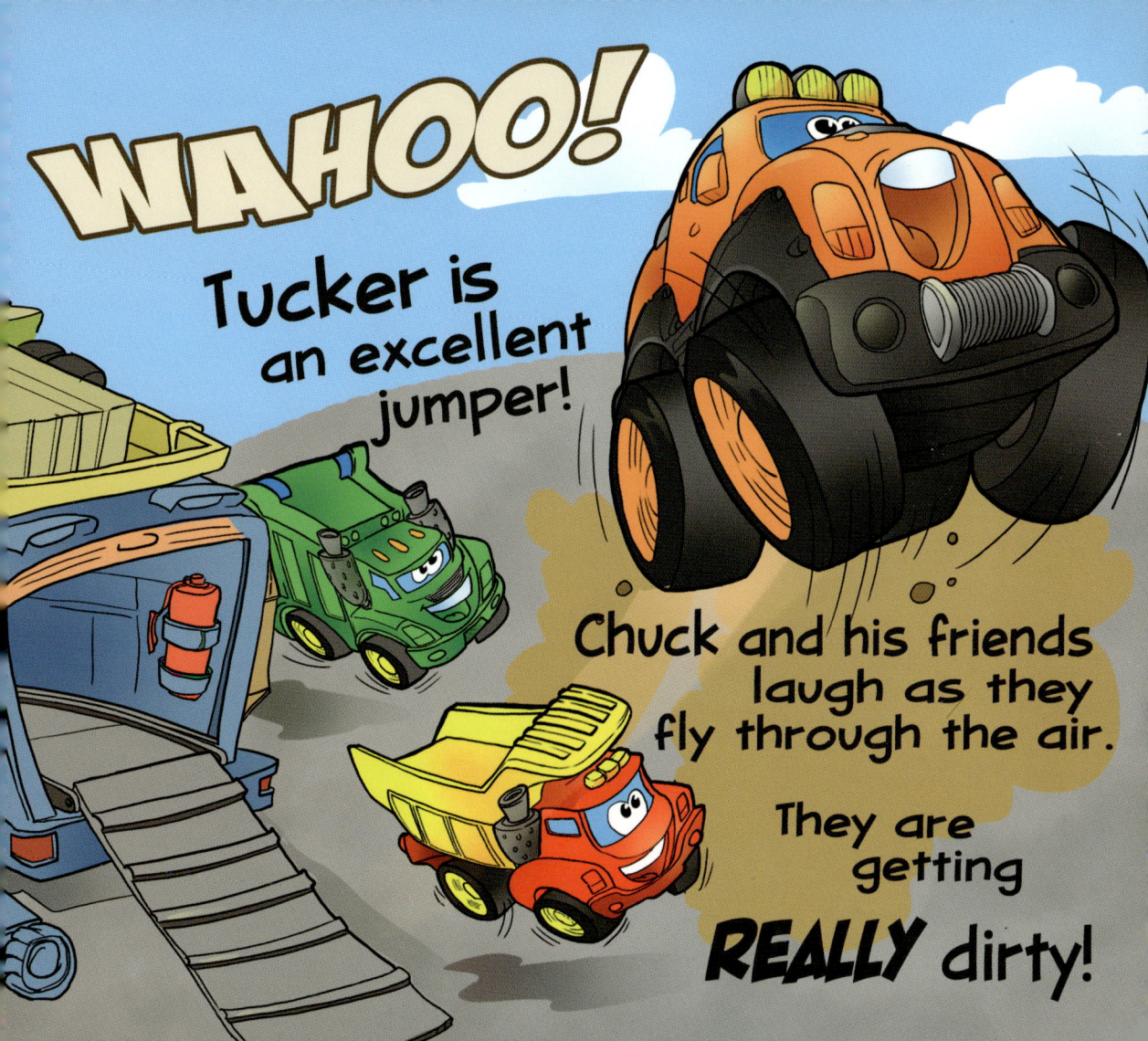

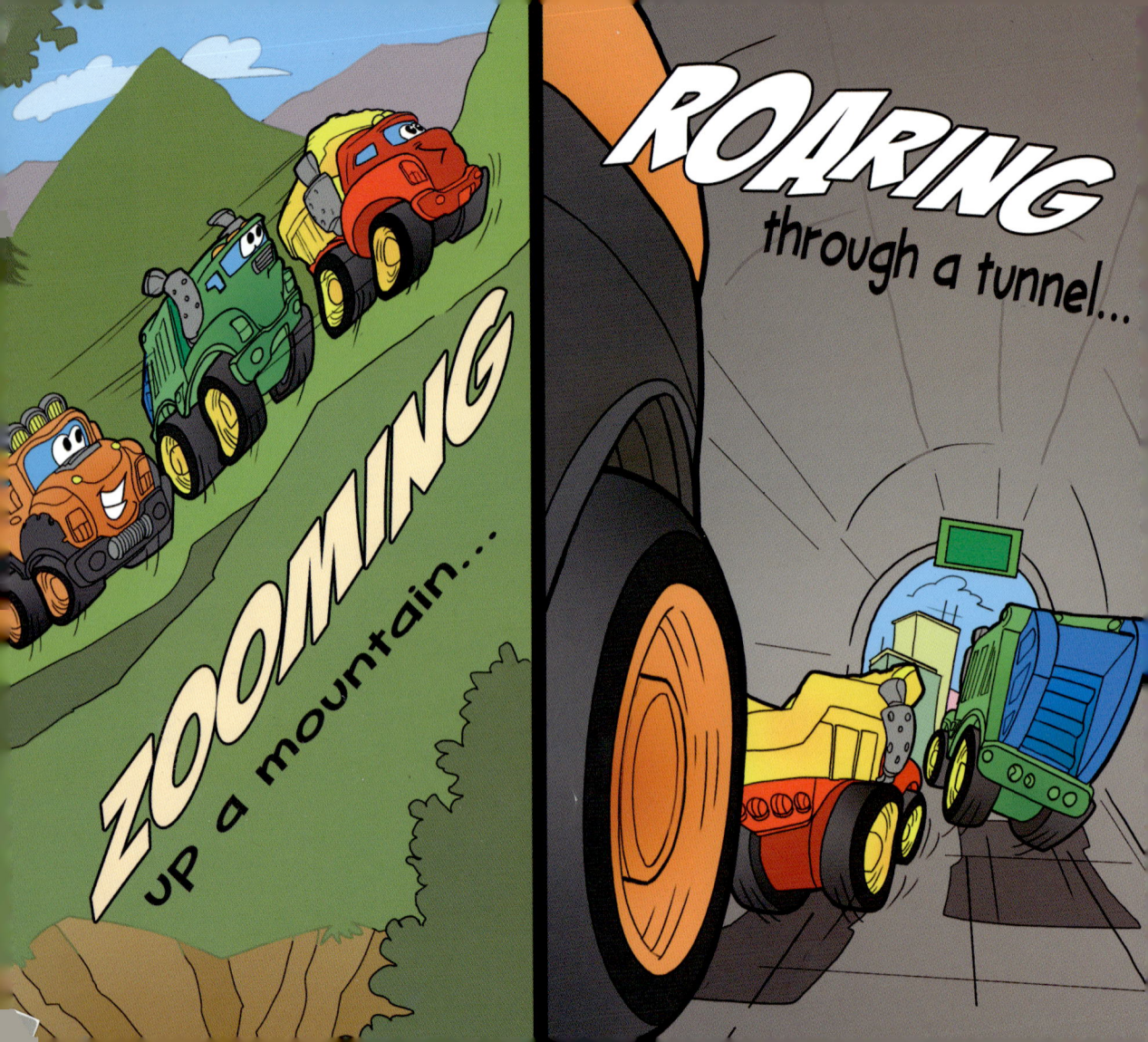

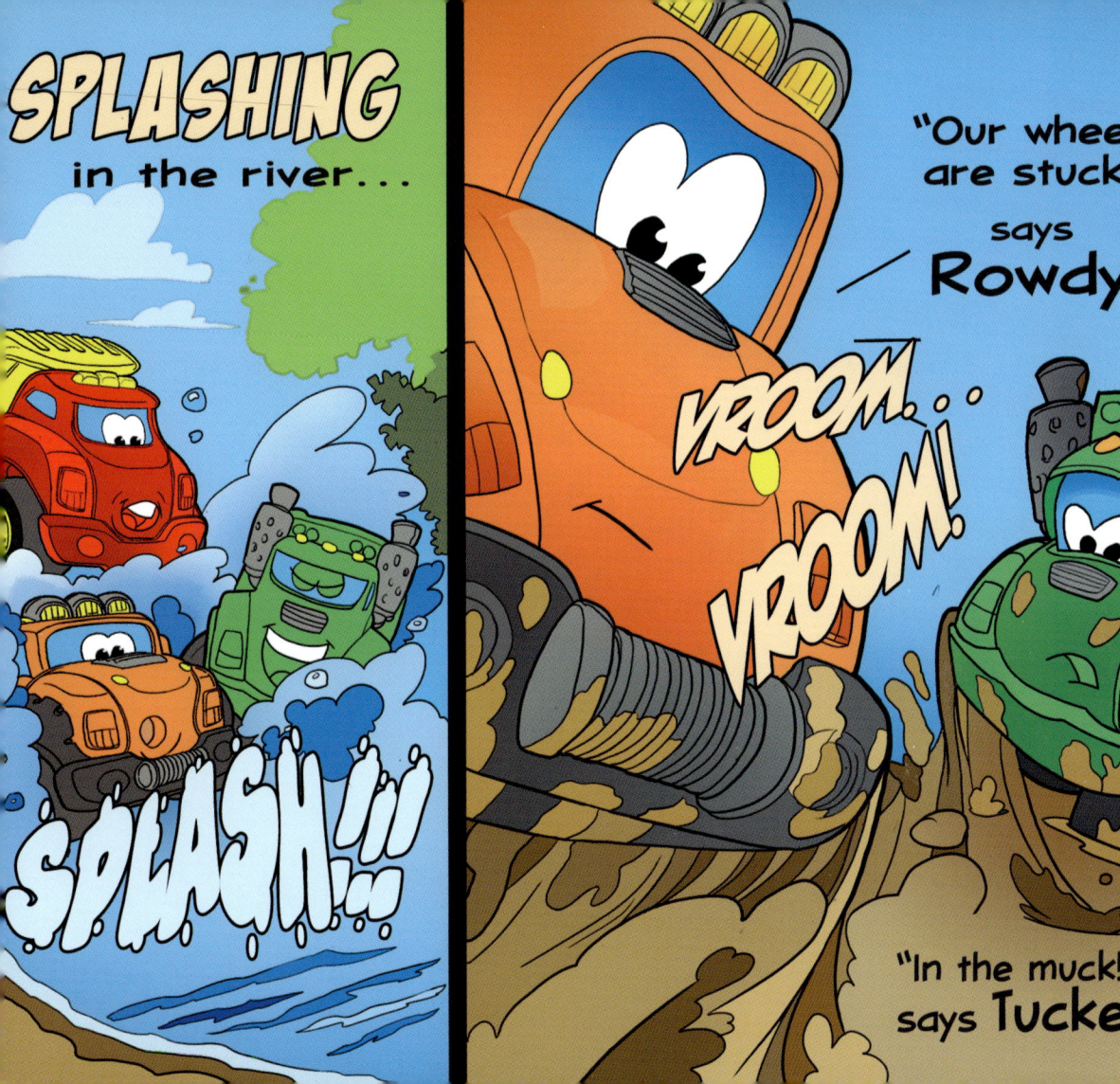

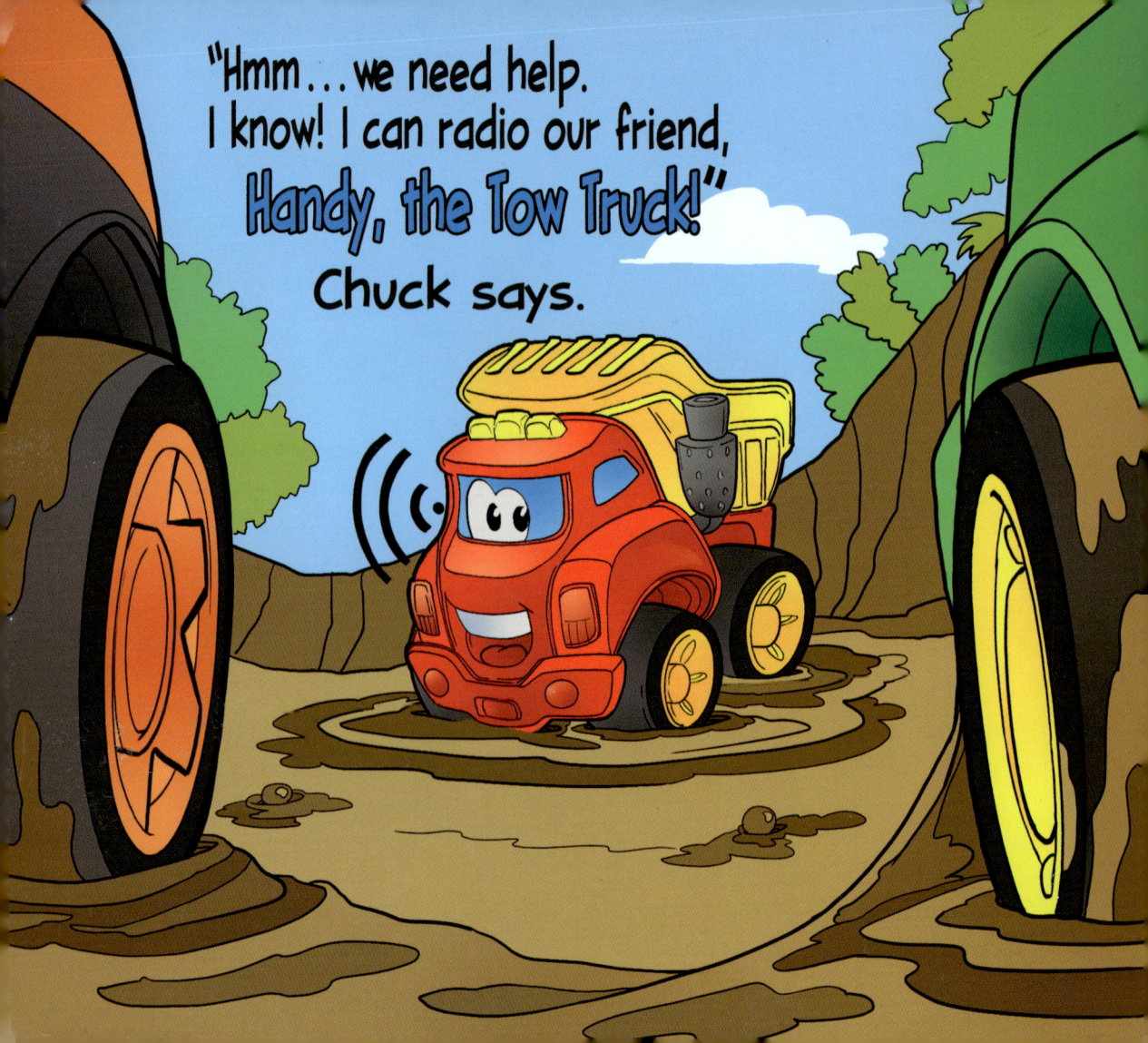

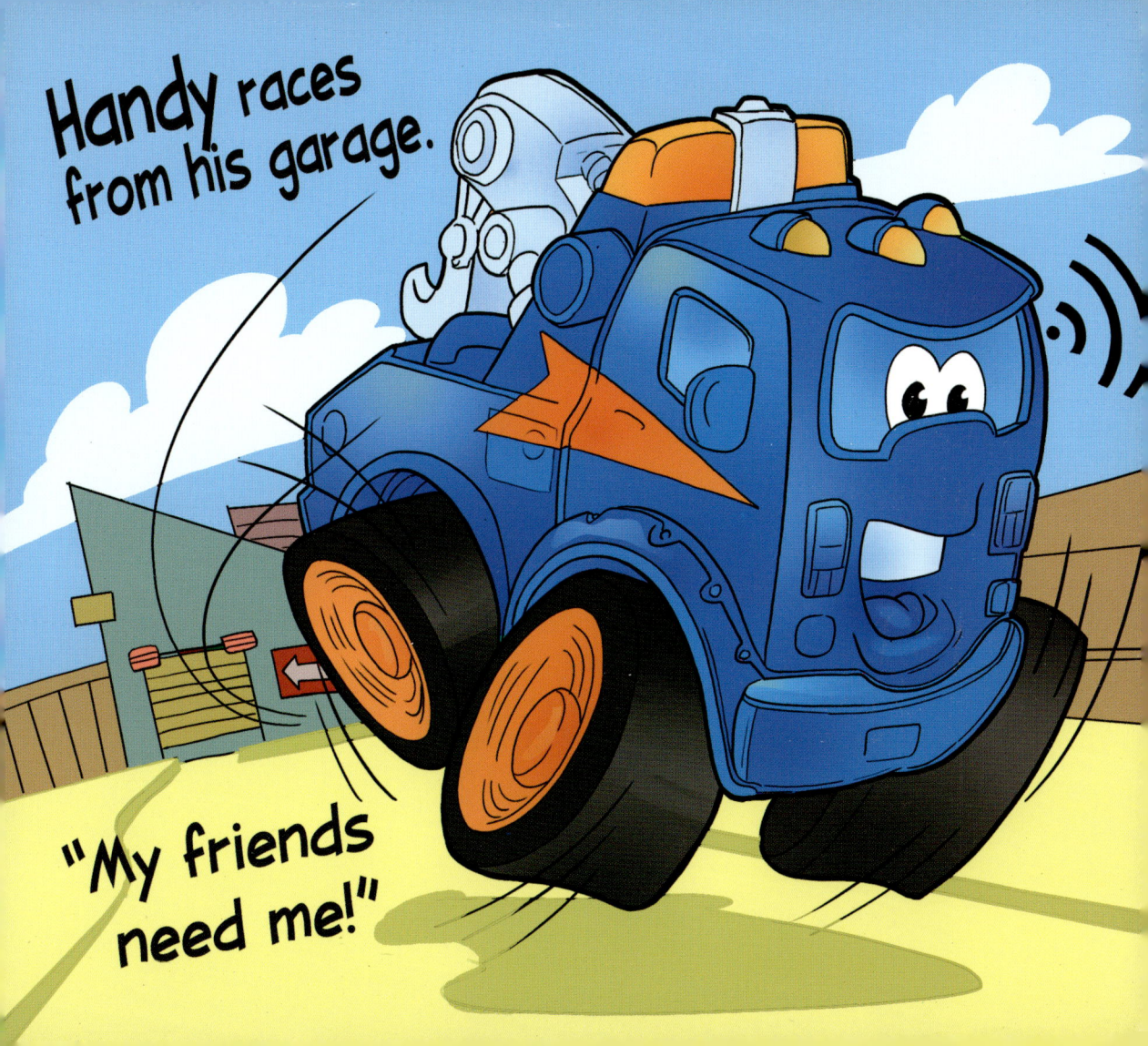

Handy uses his hook and boom
to pull them out.

They were really,
REALLY dirty now!

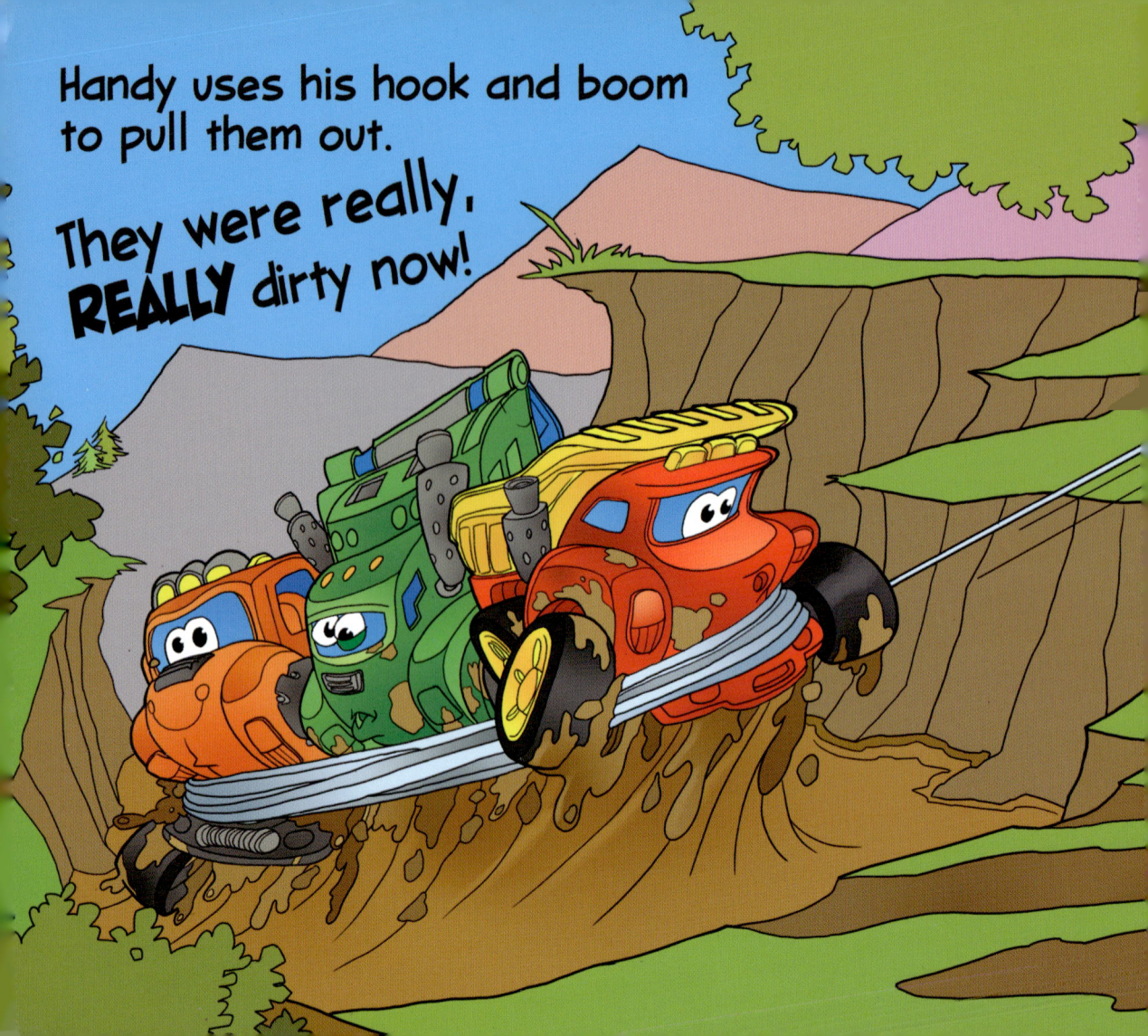

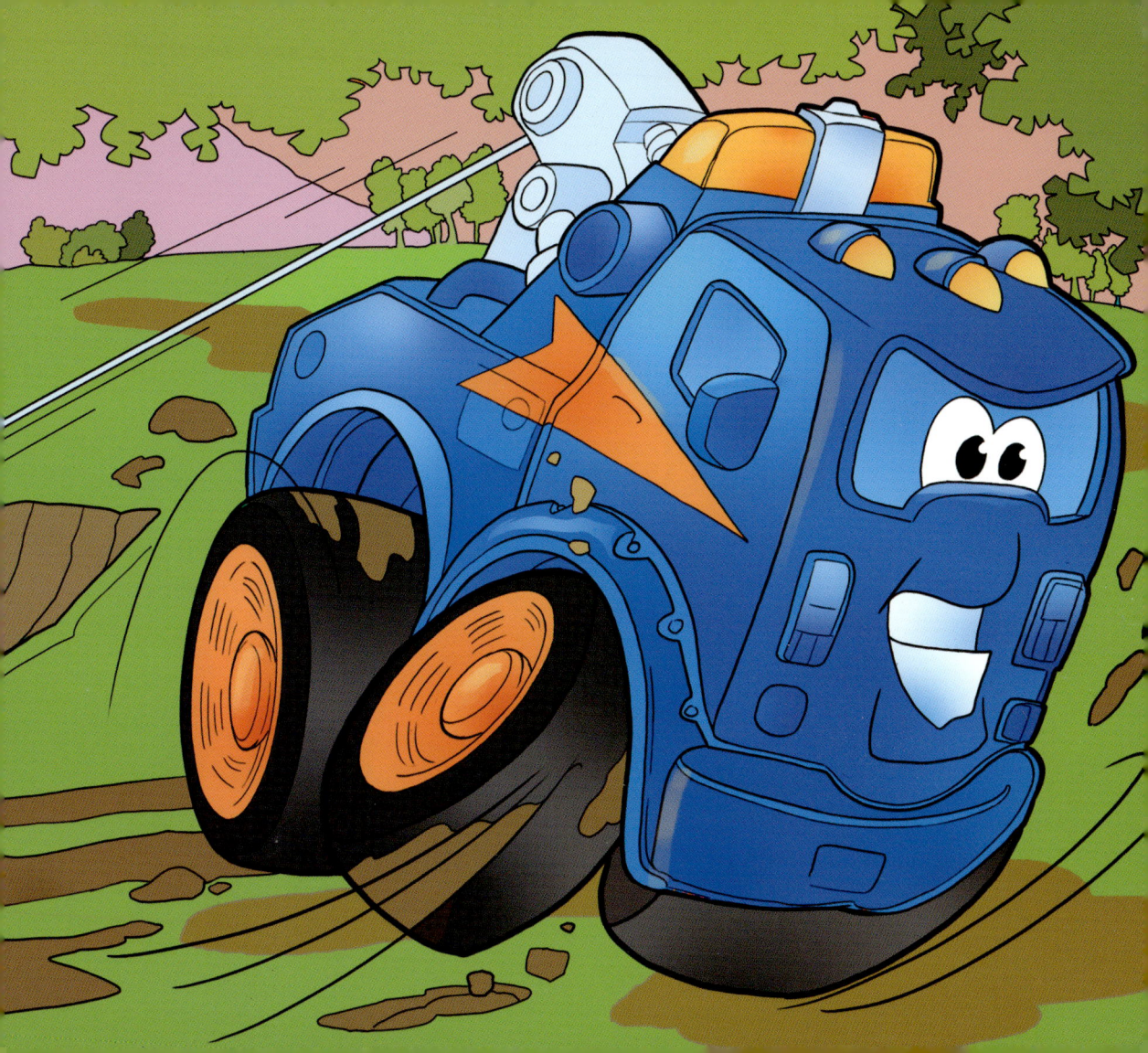

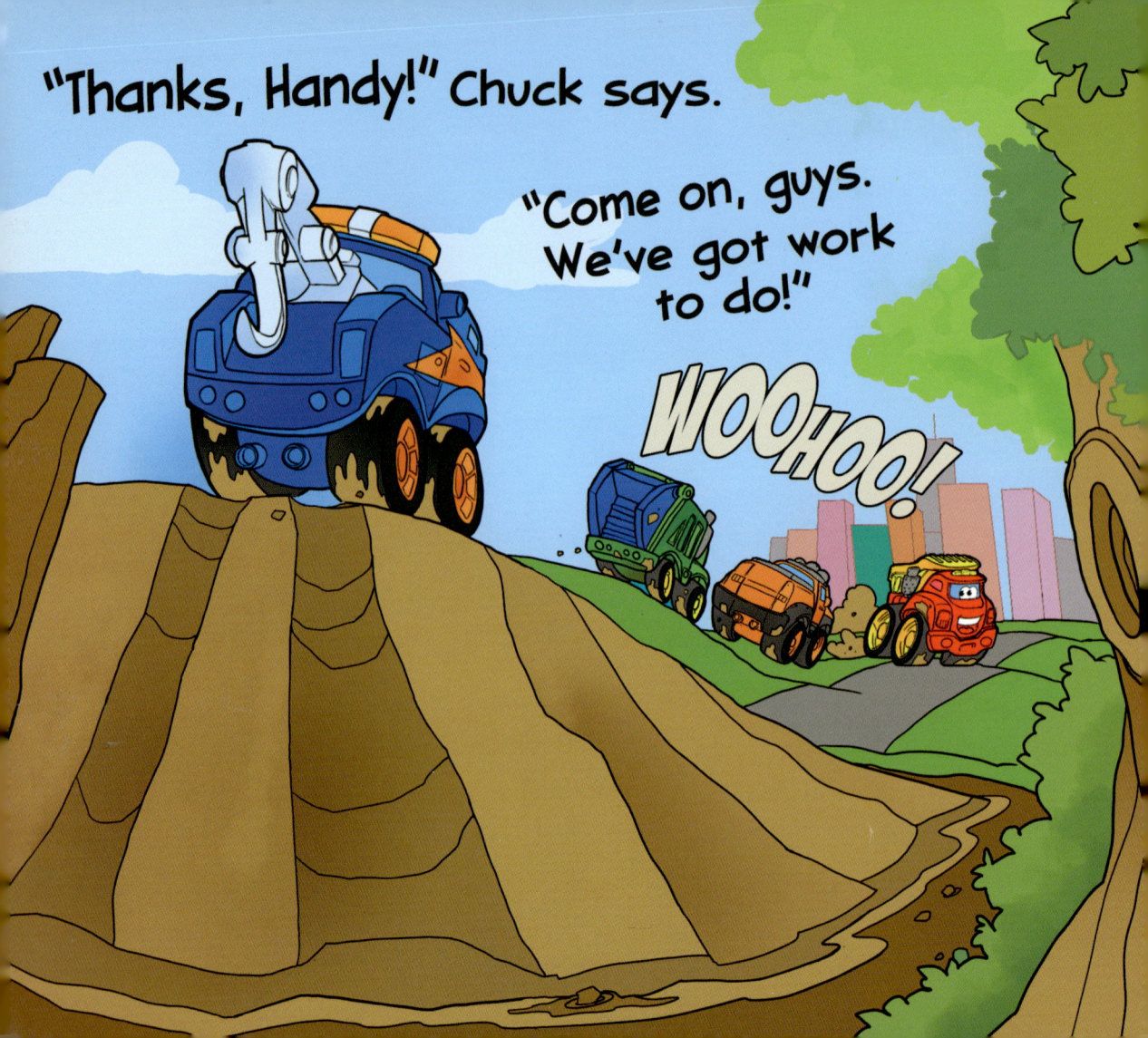

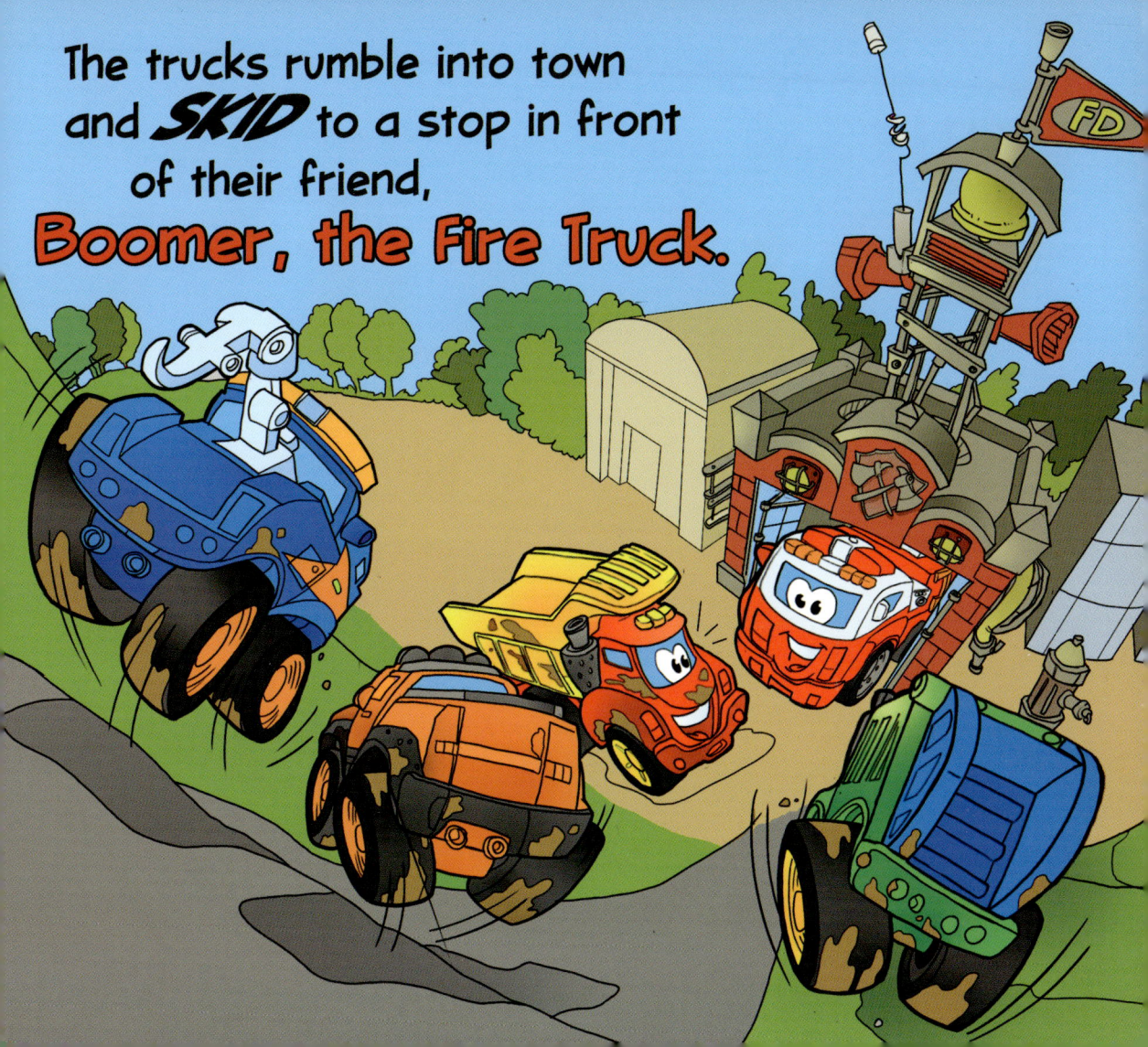

The trucks rumble into town and *SKID* to a stop in front of their friend,

Boomer, the Fire Truck.

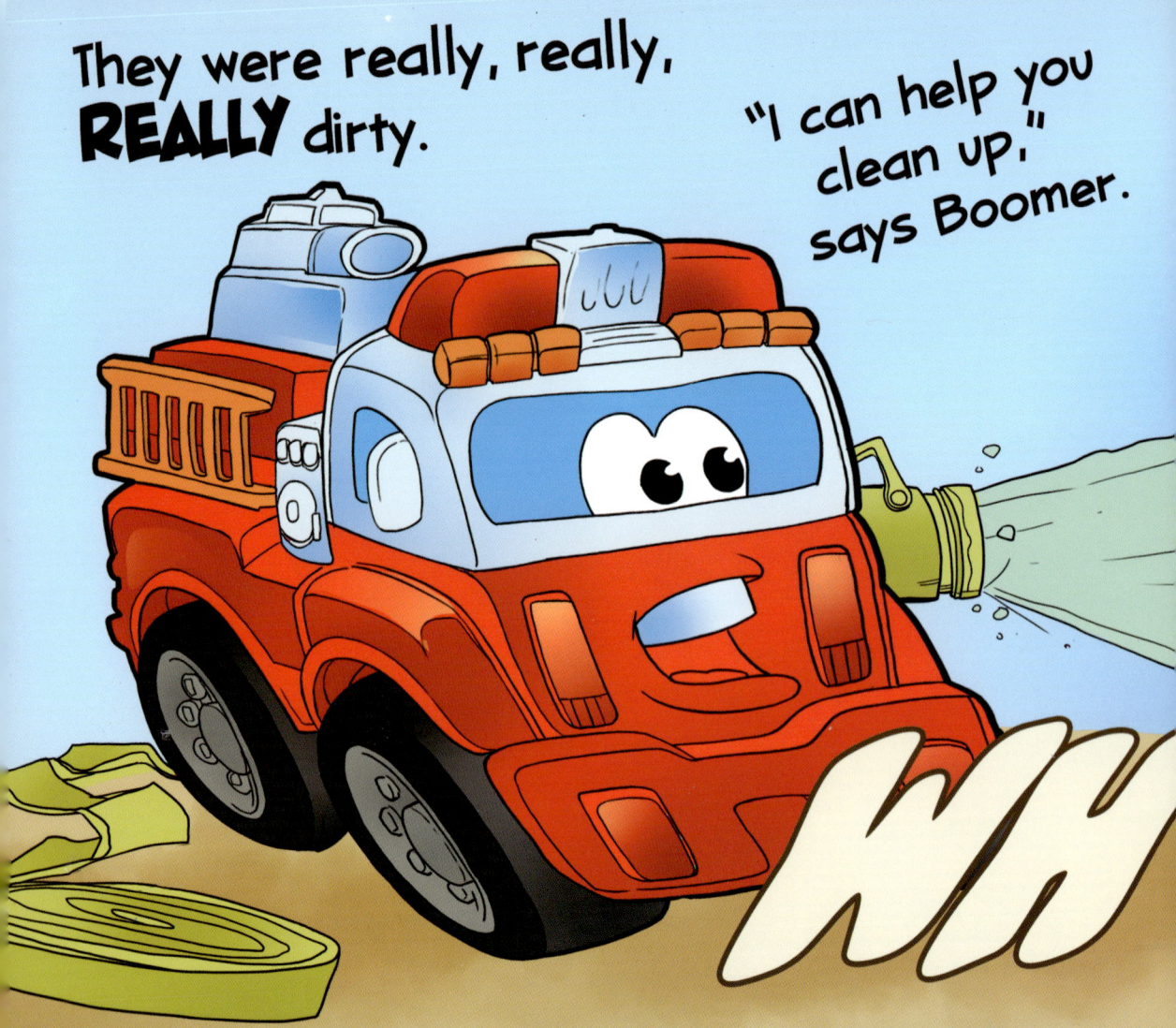

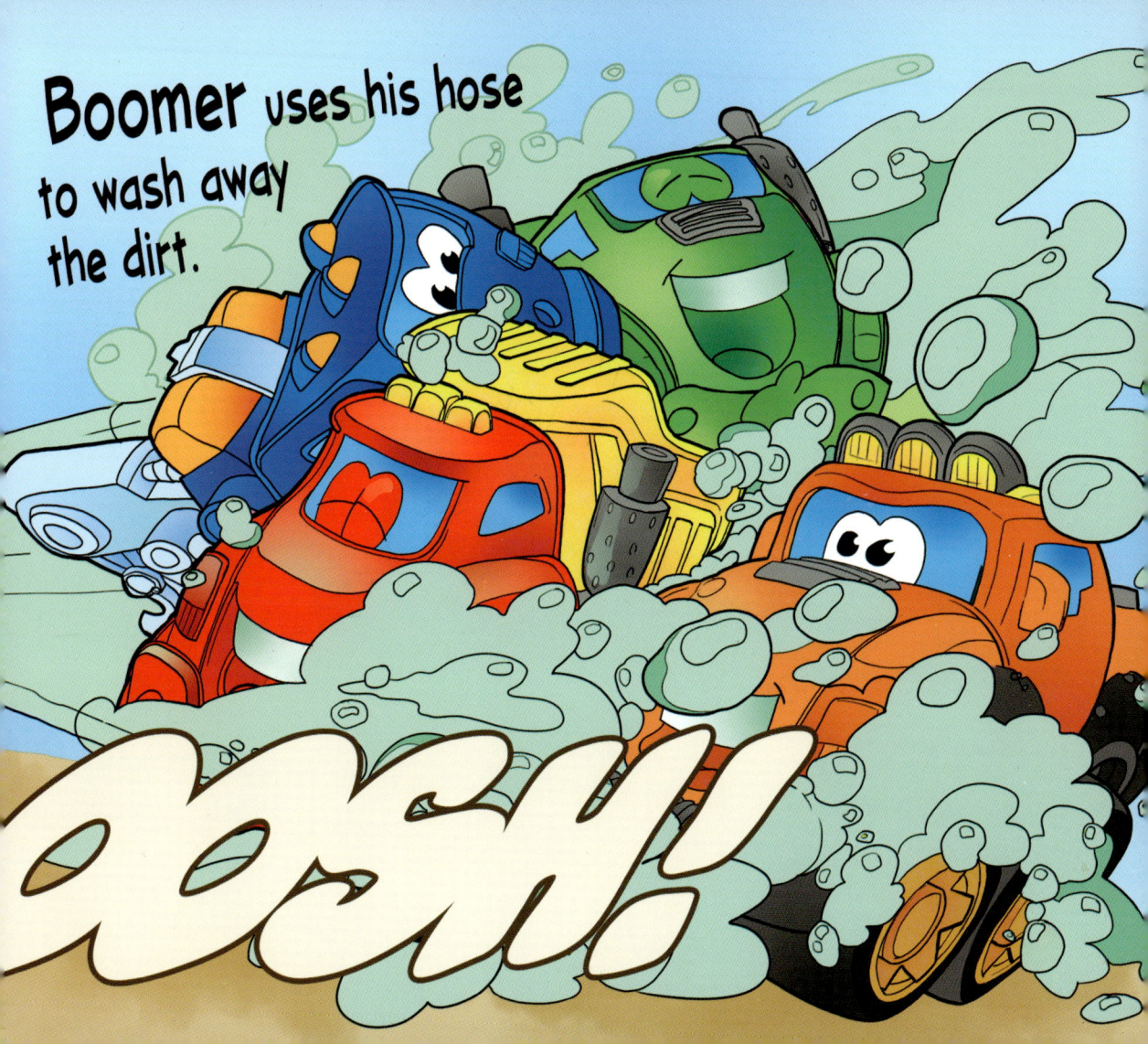

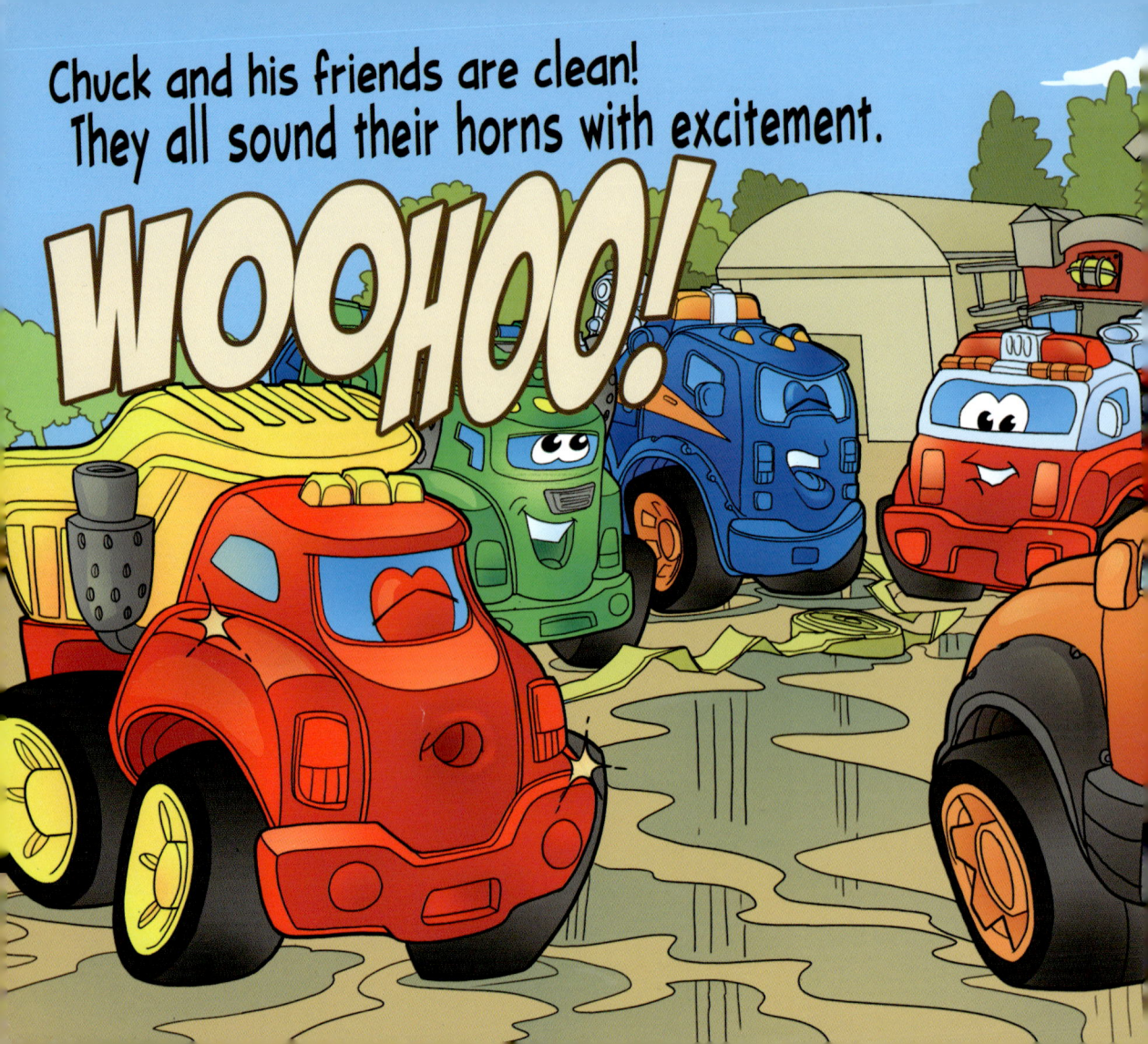

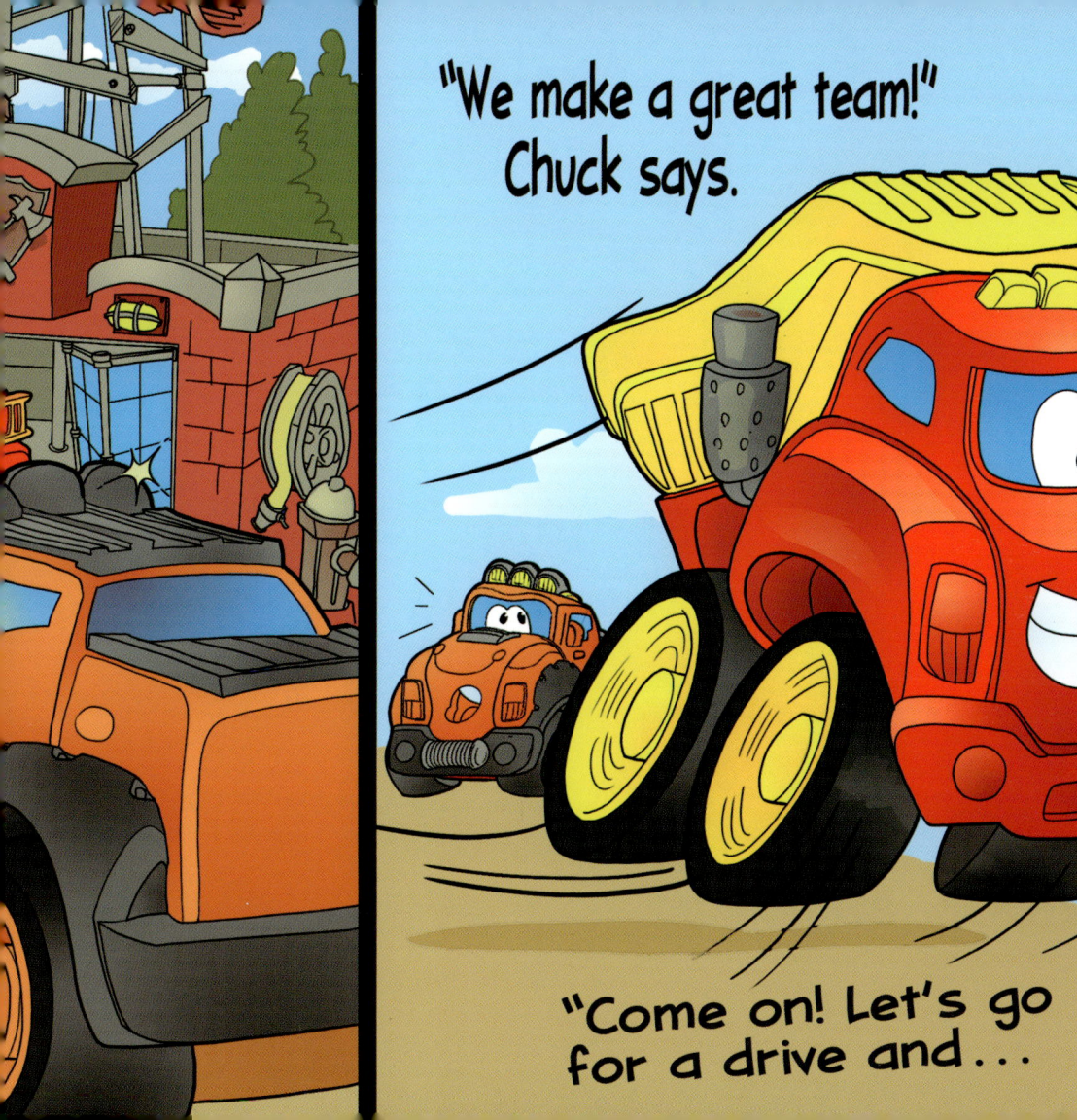

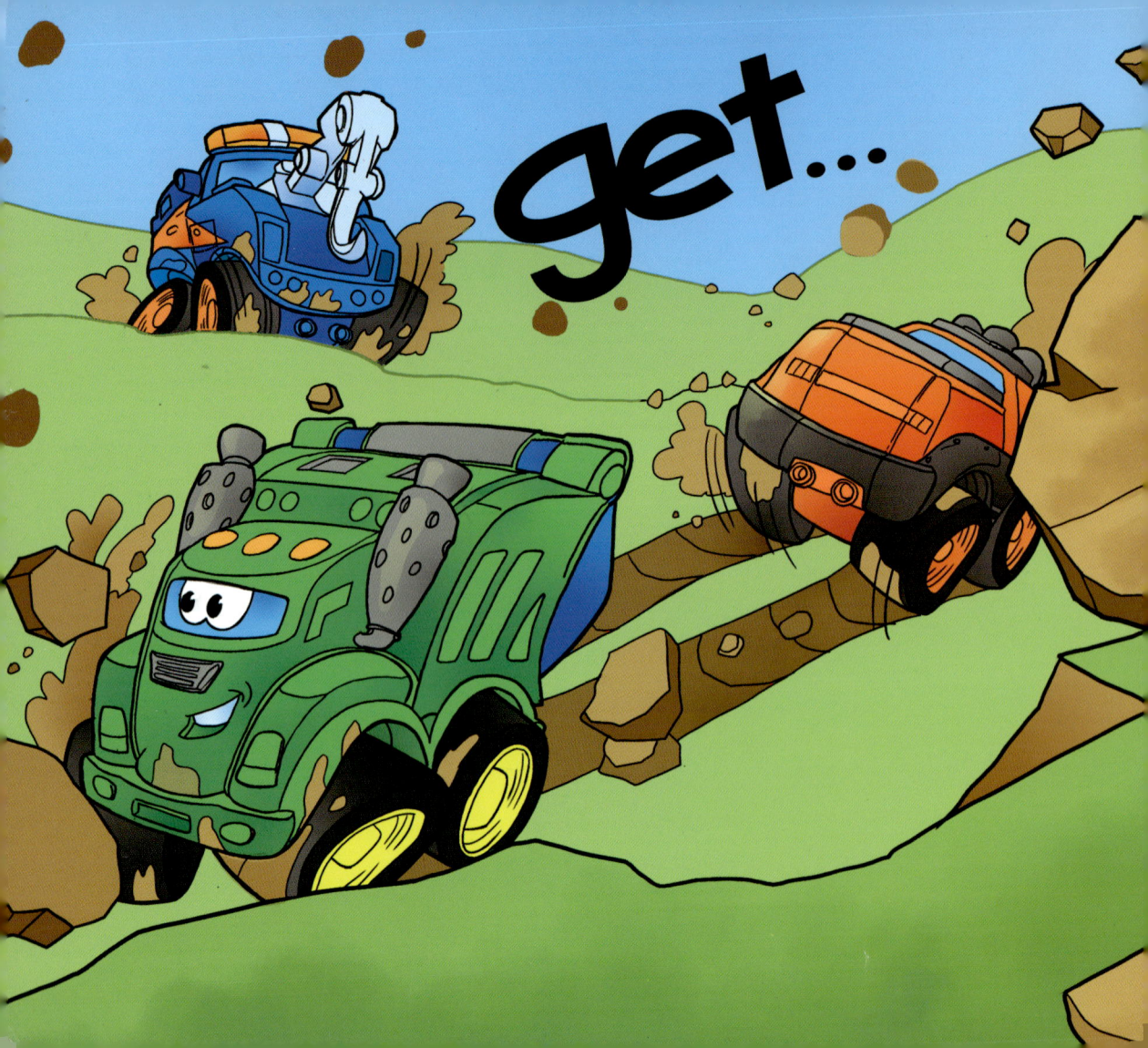

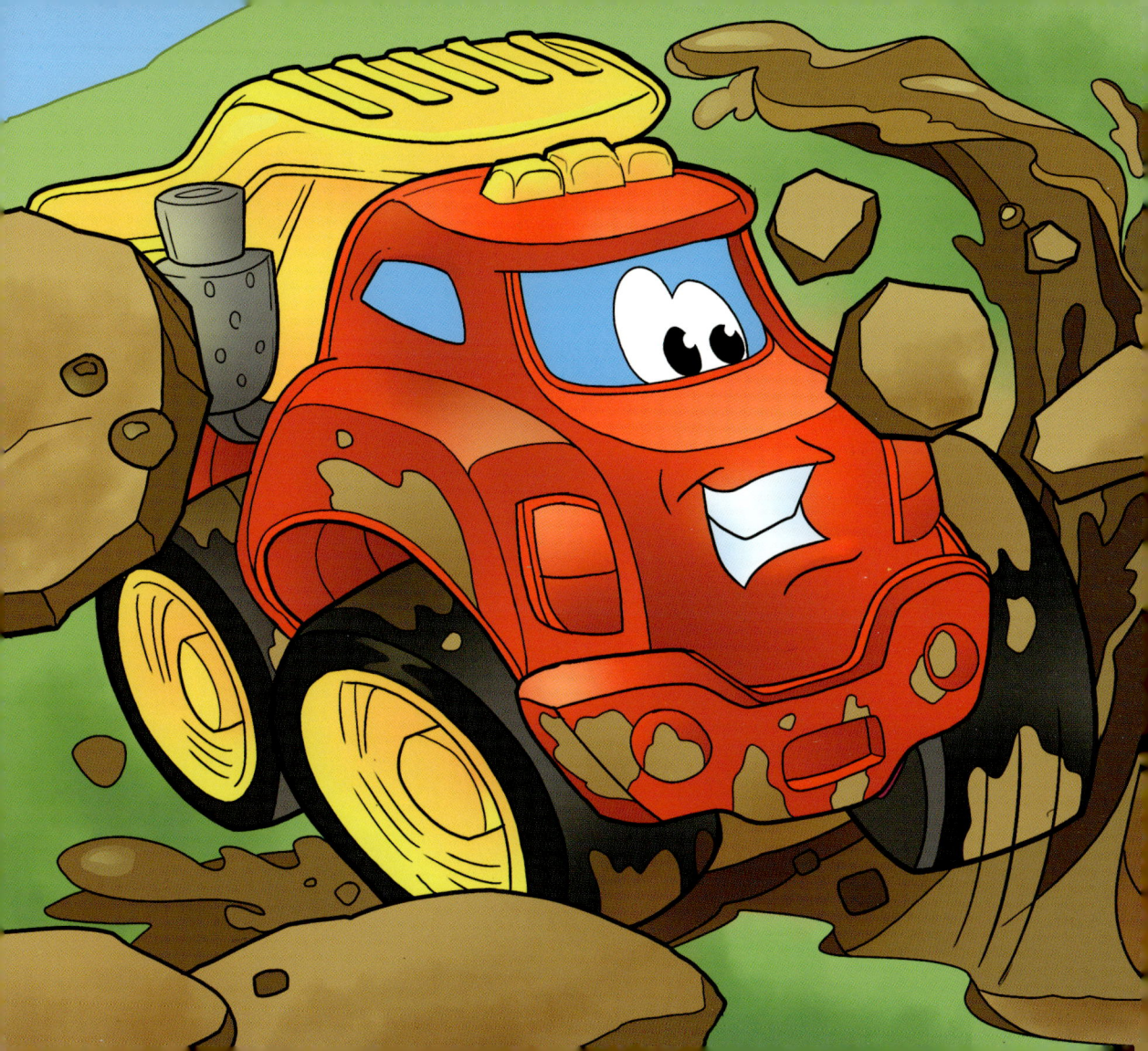

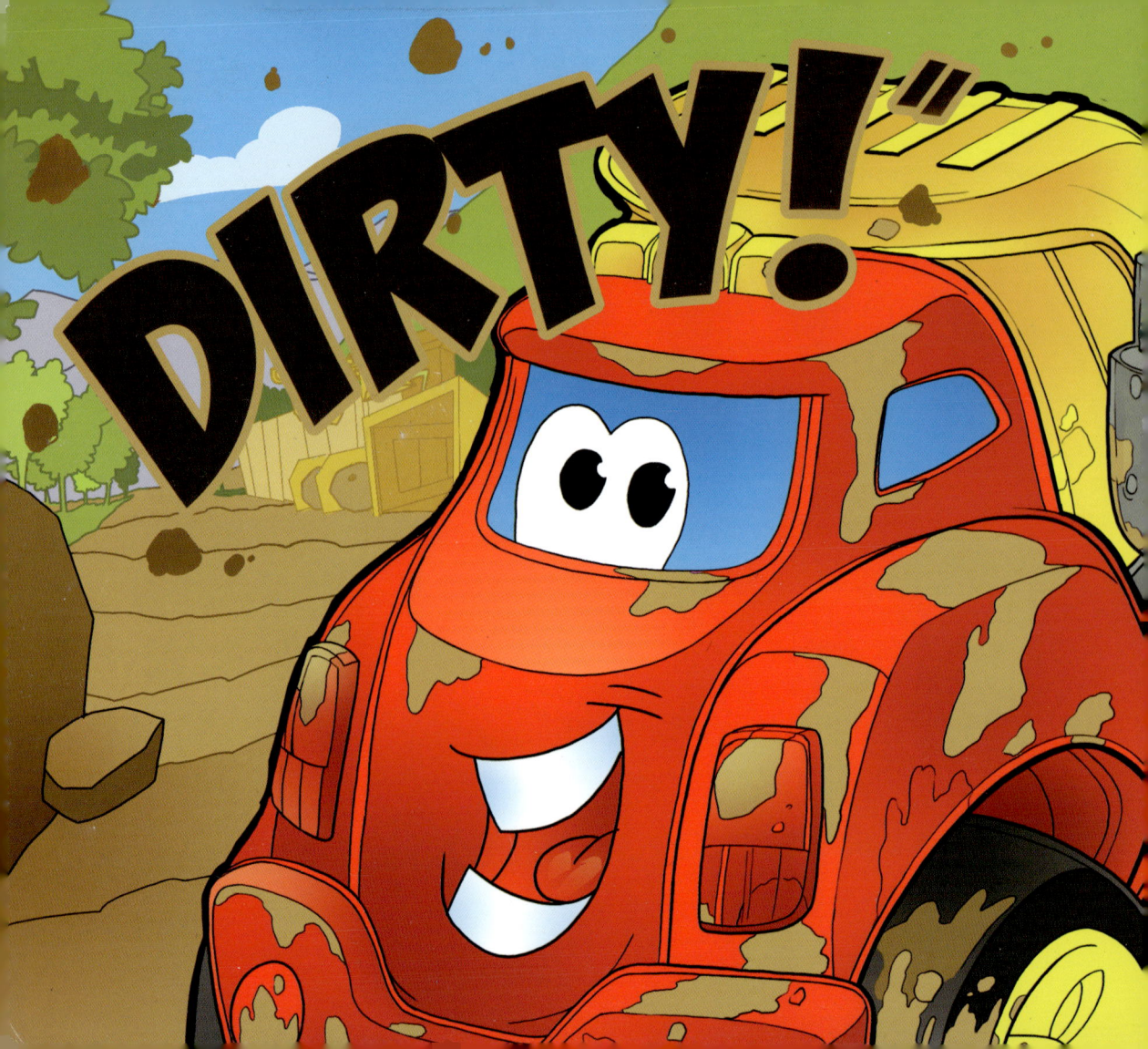